IN HAWAII

Sue Carabine

Illustrations by
Shauna Mooney Kawasaki

Gibbs Smith, Publisher

First Edition
07 06 05 04 03   5 4 3 2 1

Published by
Gibbs Smith, Publisher
P.O. Box 667
Layton, Utah 84041

1-800-748-5439 orders
www.gibbs-smith.com

Edited by Linda Nimori
Designed and produced by Mary Ellen Thompson,
  TTA Design
Printed and bound in China

ISBN 1-58685-272-8

'Twas the night before Christmas,
St. Nick couldn't wait
To treat Mama and visit
the great Aloha State.

'Twas his most favorite place
in this wonderful world—
And picturing it now
made his snow-white beard curl!

Mama always supported him,
never complained,
Standing firmly beside him
in sun, snow, and rain.

So Santa came up with
this awesome surprise
To spend Christmas on Oahu
and lush Molokai.

After filling the stockings,
they'd travel around,
Visit each lovely island,
enjoy the sweet sounds.

In Hawaii, at Christmas,
music rings through the air;
Guitars and ukuleles
are strummed with great care.

So when his sweet wife
came to kiss him goodbye,
He lifted her gently,
sat her down by his side.

"Oh, Papa, you stop that!"
she gleefully giggled,
"But you're coming," Nick chuckled,
as his round belly jiggled.

"A trip to the islands
I've got planned for you,
Shall we start in Waikiki
or Honolulu?"

She couldn't believe it
as they soared on their way
Through skies filled with stars
in their toy-laden sleigh!

They lightly touched down
at a market outdoors,
In a place called Lihue,
on Kauai, of course!

Nick hopped down, then whispered
to a smiling young man.
Mama heard him say,
"Load them on top, if you can."

In the blink of an eyelid,
their sparkling bright rig
Was filled high with treats—
and a squealing pink pig!

There was coconut pudding,
fruit cake and lumpia,
with sushi and poi,
as well as manapua.

Nick noticed the puzzled look
on Mama's face,
"We must visit a family
in Kaneohe, with haste.

"Their dad lost his job,"
Santa said, with a sigh.
"We must hurry along now
as Christmas draws nigh."

They flew to Oahu,
landed right in the yard
Of this sweet family
who was struggling so hard.

here were squeals of bright laughter
and shrieks of delight,
As parents and kids viewed
this wonderful sight!

Then Dad, Nick, and reindeer
all started to dig
An underground pit
to slow-roast the pig.

When the luau was ready,
the table was spread
For friends, mom, and children,
with Dad at the head.

Then Santa and Mama,
with smiles, waved goodbye,
And continued their journey
into the night sky.

They filled all the stockings
in Honolulu,
Mama wearing a traditional,
long bright-red mu'umu'u.

Flying over Pearl Harbor,
they were able to see,
U.S. ships and memorials
in great majesty.

With reverence they thought
of that day in December,
Then silently promised
they'd always remember.

The USS Missouri,
Arizona, Bowfin
Still inspire all visitors
with the spirit to win!

"Thank you, dear Papa,
for bringing me here,"
Mama whispered into
her beloved Nick's ear.

As she glanced at dear Santa,
her face filled with awe,
At the wonderful acts
of great kindness she saw.

Then, approaching Molokai,
Santa spoke of a note
He'd received from this island.
A little child wrote:

"Dear Santa, please listen
to my desperate plea,
I must teach my young sisters
to hula with me

"And perform in a program
for our neighborhood.
But, to teach them the hula,
well, I'm not very good!"

"We need to assist her,"
cried dear old St. Nick,
"Are you willing to help me,
dear Mama, and quick?"

She laughed as they landed
on the balmy seashore
Where, patiently waiting,
were the sisters—all four.

They quickly made sure
Nick and Mama were dressed
In bracelets and leglets,
grass skirts and the rest.

Leis circled their necks
and were placed on their heads.
(They were very becoming
in this new set of threads!)

"Come along, my dear children,
and do it this way,"
Called Santa, whose broad hips
had started to sway.

As they watched Santa hula,
their eyes opened wide,
Then they followed his lead
and all swayed side to side.

Mrs. Claus, who was cheering
and shaking with mirth,
Said, "Papa, this way
you'll lose pounds from your girth!"

But Nick taught them well
and his dear Mama knew it.
The girls cried, "Thanks, Santa,
we knew you could do it!"

St. Nick and his sweetheart
just hated to leave,
But there were so many things
they must do Christmas Eve.

The islands of Maui,
Hawaii, Lanai—
They were longing to go there
as Christmas drew nigh.

Hawaii's volcano
in its national park
Spewed incredible colors
in the velvety dark.

"We must leave here quite soon,"
said St. Nick to his bride.
"Have you one more wish, dear,
I may grant you tonight?"

She looked at him shyly
(this old man she adored),
Then asked, "Would you mind
if I rode a surfboard?"

This time Santa's blue eyes
grew round with surprise.
"Of course, you may do that,
and I'll be by your side!

"It so happens I've got
balsa boards here on hand
For soldiers and sailors
in the Pacific Command!"

Do you think that they'd teach me?"
she eyed Nick again.
"My dear, I can't wait
till I see you 'hang ten'!"

On Boogie- and surfboards,
Her wish was soon granted:
Mama rode ten-foot waves
with her feet firmly planted.

So that's how it happened:
with the help of great surfers
St. Nick and his Mama
rode waves that were perfect!

From Kauai to Hilo,
Wai'nae to Kailua,
The folks of Hawaii
signed shaka, "Aloha."

Then our jolly old couple
and reindeer took flight,
Calling "Mele Kalikimaka!
To you all a good night!"